Santa's Musical Elves

By Lillian Webb Taylor

Strategic Book Publishing
New York, New York

Copyright © 2009
All rights reserved by Lillian Webb Taylor

No part of this book may be reproduced or transmitted in any form or by any means, graphic, electronic, or mechanical, including photocopying, recording, taping, or by any information storage retrieval system, without the permission, in writing, from the publisher.

Strategic Book Publishing
An imprint of Writers Literary & Publishing Services, Inc.
845 Third Avenue, 6th Floor – 6016
New York, NY 10022
http://www.strategicbookpublishing.com

ISBN: 978-1-60860-146-2   1-60860-146-3

Printed in the United States of America

Illustrations art, book cover art and book layout by
kalpart team - www.kalpart.com

For TRT, MKT and AET
with my love

Acknowledgements

In appreciation

Dr. John Brewton
Mrs. Pauline Milner
Mr. Richard Rose

There's a dear old man named Santa;
he wears a suit of red.
And every Christmas night,
I'm told, eight reindeer guide his sled.

He goes to every house in town;
he never misses one.
He brings all the children lots of joy
and so much fun.

His little elves will help him;
they make toys all year long.
They like to work for Santa
and each one can sing a song.

"Tra la de dah," sings Ellie Elf.
"Tra la de dah, de dah!"

"Boom boom, varoom,"
croons Eddie Elf.

"Boom boom, varoom, kaboom!"

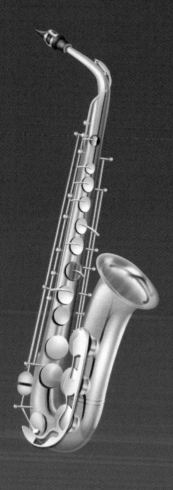

Then Santa says,
"Good music, elves,
you know just what to say!
Let's get our instruments
out today
so we can sing AND play!"

So Ernie Elf strums his guitar,
his music fills the room,

"Toodle-ee, toodle-ah,
toodle-oh, ho ho!"

He loves that happy tune!

Then Essie Elf says, "Back to work,
we have so much to do.
The children sent their lists to us;
each list we must review!"

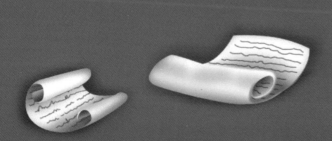

Ava wants a dollhouse
and Trevor wants space guns.
Of course, I know they'll get them
'cause dear Santa loves each one.

Kate surely needs a bicycle
to speed her on her way.
The many things from Santa are
for play and happy days!

There are toys in the sled
for each child in this world,
dolls and games for
each boy and each girl.

So, if you are good
the whole year long
and do not fuss or do
anything wrong,

Santa will bring all the
good girls and boys
lots and lots of
brand-new toys.

LaVergne, TN USA
06 November 2009
163357LV00003B

9 781608 601462